Animal Train

by *Elizabeth Roberts*

Illustrations by
Ben D. Williams

MERRIGOLD PRESS • NEW YORK

Text © 1952 Merrigold Press. Illustrations © 1952 by Ben D. Williams. All rights reserved. Printed in the U.S.A. No part of this book may be reproduced or copied in any form without written permission from the publisher. All trademarks are the property of Merrigold Press, Racine, Wisconsin 53402. ISBN 0-307-17705-X MCMXCIV

Clickety-click, clickety-click went the animal train, hurrying on its way to the zoo. *Ding-ding-dong* rang the bell and *toot-toot-toot* tootled the whistle.

And the animals heard and the engineer heard and the brakeman heard and the conductor heard. But what the engineer didn't know and what the brakeman didn't know—but what the animals did know—was that the giraffe had chewed a big hole in the roof of their car.

And out climbed the giraffe, and
out climbed the elephant——

out climbed the brown bear, and
out climbed a band of monkeys——

a monkey with a horn,
a monkey with a drum,
a monkey with a fife.

Tootety-toot
went the horn.

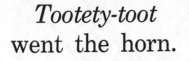

Drumity-drum
went the drum.

Fifety-fife
went the fife.

The giraffe went hippety-hop-
ping along one car after another,
the length of the train.

The elephant waltzed behind
him, and the bear danced and
turned somersaults in rhythm
with the monkey band.

And the train went *clickety-click, clickety-click* over the rails.

Then up popped the conductor and yelled till he was red in the face. Up popped the brakeman and shook his fist till he was red in the face. And the engineer blew the whistle till the engine was red in the face.

But the monkeys played on, the giraffe hippety-hopped, and the elephant waltzed, and the bear danced and turned somersaults, and the train went *clickety-click, clickety-click.*

Then down went the conductor, and down went the brakeman. The engineer didn't blow the whistle any more, and the train didn't go *clickety-click,* *clickety-click,* fast. But it went *c-l-i-c-k-e-t-y—c-l-i-c-k-e-t-y,* very slowly.

Now, what the giraffe didn't know and what the elephant didn't know and what the bear didn't know and what the monkey band didn't know, but what the conductor did know and what the engineer did know—was that the train was entering a tunnel, a very low tunnel, just high enough for the cars to slip through.

And this is what happened: the giraffe was pushed back, the elephant was pushed back, the bear was pushed back, and the monkey band was pushed back.

And all of them, one by one, dropped through the hole which the giraffe had chewed in the roof of their car. They all dropped through the hole down into their car again.

Then the conductor and the brakeman and the engineer all worked away and nailed up the hole the giraffe had made.

Then they fed the animals their supper. And the animals ate their suppers and went to sleep.

And the train went *clickety-click, clickety-click* over the rails once more.